1939-1945
WORLD WAR TWO

AUTHORS

Paolo Crippa (23 April 1978) has cultivated his passion for Italian history since high school. His research interests are focused mainly in the field of military history and in particular on italian armored units from the 30s until the end of World War II. In 2006 he published his first volume, "I Reparti Corazzati della Repubblica Sociale Italiana 1943/1945", the first organic research carried out and published in Italy on the subject. In 2007 he published "Duecento Volti della R.S.I." and in 2011 " Un anno con il 27° Reggimento Artiglieria Legnano". He regularly contributes to several journals: Milites, New Historica, SGM - World War II, Batailes & Blindes, Armoured Vehicles and history of the twentieth century, Mezzi Corazzati, both as an author, or in collaboration with other researchers. He published with the editor Mattioli 1885 in 2014 "Italy 43 – 45 – Civil War improvised AFV's" (2014), "Italian AFV's of the Civil War 1943 - 1945" (2015) and "Italy 43 – 45 – AFV's and MV's of co-belligerent units" (2018).

Carlo Cucut was born in Nole (TO) in 1955. He cultivated a passion for history as a boy and over the years has deepened this interest by dedicating himself to historical research. He published articles in the italian magazines: "Storia del XX Secolo", "Storie & Battaglie", "Milites" and "Ritterkreuz". He published various volumes for Marvia Edizioni: "Penne Nere on the eastern border. History of the Alpini's Regiment "Tagliamento" 1943-1945 ", winner of the "De Cia" Award; "Attilio Viziano. Memories of a war correspondent "; "Armed Forces of RSI on the eastern front"; "Armed Forces of RSI on the Western Front"; "Armed Forces of RSI on the Gothic Line"; "Alpini in the City of Rijeka 1944-1945". For the Trentino Modeling Group he published "The armed forces of RSI 1943-1945. Land forces ".

PUBLISHING'S NOTES

LICENSES COMMONS

For a complete list of Soldiershop titles please contact Luca Cristini Editore on our website: www.soldiershop.com or www.cristinieditore.com. E-mail: info@soldiershop.com

Title: **ITALIAN ARMORED UNITS IN THE BALKANS 1941-1945** Code.: WTW-007 EN
By Carlo Cucut & Paolo Crippa.
ISBN code: 978-88-93275101 first edition October 2019
English text Nr. of images: 120 layout: 7x10 inch (177,8x254mm) Cover & Art Design: Luca S. Cristini

WITNESS TO WAR (SOLDIERSHOP) is a trademark of Luca Cristini Editore, via Orio, 35/4 - 24050 Zanica (BG) ITALY.

WITNESS TO WAR

ITALIAN ARMORED UNITS IN THE BALKANS 1941 - 1945

PHOTOS & IMAGES FROM WORLD WARTIME ARCHIVES

PAOLO CRIPPA - CARLO CUCUT

Contents

INTRODUCTION

As early as the 1930s the Fascist regime had begun to develop an expansionist project aimed at controlling the Mediterranean and the Balkans. The Kingdom of Italy had already had the possession of the Dodecanese Islands since 1912 and since 1926 the protectorate over Albania and, with these assumptions, after the occupation of the Kingdom of Albania in 1939 and the outbreak of the Second World War the following year , Mussolini concentrated his efforts against Greece, starting in October 1940 a disastrous military campaign, which forced the German Reich to a massive intervention in support of the Italian Armed Forces. The Italian military weakness thus transformed what could be considered for Italy a "parallel" war to secure control of Albania, Greece and Yugoslavia, in a war subordinate to Germany.

The Greek Campaign determined the division of the territories into areas of occupation and also in Yugoslavia the Fascist regime had to accept a shared occupation with Germany, Hungary and Bulgaria. While in the territories annexed to the Kingdom of Italy the entire pre-existing political and administrative system was dismantled, in Croatia and Montenegro the Regime granted a limited form of independence, badly accepted by the local population. The occupation of the Balkans by the Axis forces and the consequent destruction of the pre-existing political order created the conditions for the explosion of ethnic wars and the beginning of resistance, which was violently fought through a brutal repression and a series of military operations, especially German, which aimed to eradicate the partisan movement.

The Armistice of 8th September 1943 forced the Italian Commands to make choices in the field, without having clear the situation or the consequences of their choices, at the mercy of the Germans and the partisans, all interested in grabbing arms. In some cases, the Germans asked the Italian Commands to continue the struggle with Germany: around 94,000 men joined immediately. These would have been joined by more than another 100,000 Italian soldiers, driven by the harsh conditions of imprisonment in which the Germans had forced them. Most units in the Balkans decided to surrender to the Germans, while another part instead chose to fight with the partisan movement.

THE ITALIAN CAMPAIGNS IN THE BALKANS 1939 - 1941

Occupation of Albany

Following the rejection of the ultimatum, sent on 25th March 1939 by Rome, by King Zog I, on 7th April 1939 began the military occupation of the Kingdom of Albania by the Kingdom of Italy. The first wave of the Oltre-Mare Tirana Expeditionary Corps (OMT) hit the Albanian territory divided into four columns, which landed in San Giovanni di Medua, Santi Quaranta, Valona and Durazzo, encountering little resistance from the weak unitts of the Albanian Army, accompanied in some cases by gendarmes and civilians. Durazzo was conquered after only 5 hours of combat, on the morning of 8th April Tirana was in Italian hands, in the evening Scutari fell after hours of battle between the streets of the city. On 12th April, the fighting ceased and Albania was entirely in the hands of Italian units. King Zog with his family and the Albanian government fled to Greece and was forced into exile. Albania ceased de facto to exist as an independent state. In total, about 22,000 Italians who landed in Albania and occupied the country. Among the troops of the first group destined for landing, in the column destined for the occupation of Durres, the Fast Tank Company of the 2nd Bersaglieri Regiment, equipped with L3/35 tanks, and the Light Tank Group "D'Antoni", were present. from the Battalions Carri L VIII and X of the 31st Tankers Infantry Regiment, also equipped with L3/33 and L3/35 tanks. In the column destined to Santi Quaranta was present the III Group Fast Tanks "San Giorgio", also equipped with light tanks L3/33 and L3/35. In total, over 200 light tanks were engaged in the occupation of Albania.

In the summer of 1939, the transfer to Albania of the "Centauro" Armored Division began, with the 31st Tank Regiment on four L Battalions, where, in addition to the foreseen garrison's duties, it completed the training between the unitts. In the summer of 1940, the 31st was moved to the Klisura - Tepeleni area, in the sector of Epirus, in anticipation of the start of operations against Greece. During the occupation, the 1st Frontier Tanks Company, belonging to the "Guardia alla Frontiera" (GaF), equipped with obsolete Fiat 3000/21 and Fiat 3000/30 tanks, was transferred to the area of Scutari, in northern Albania on the border with Yugoslavia.

War against Greece
On 28th October 1940 hostilities began against Greece, probably the most disastrous and fatal military campaign, despite the short duration, among those conducted by the Italian Army during the Second World War. It was a badly born campaign, conducted with carelessness, ignorance of the Command, badly managed, badly organized, which, if not turned into a tragic route, was only because, once again, the Italian soldiers were able to resist in inhumane conditions to frost, to hunger, fatigue, and wounds, commanded by those few officers who honored the rank brought, they succeeded in blocking the advance of the Greek troops which by now were well within the Albanian borders. In that immense tragedy the tankers of the 31st Regiment were the first to cross the border with two columns, a main one with three L 3 Battalions and a light one with the remaining Battalion, in the valleys of the Drin and the Voiussa, with the aim of investing Kalpaki. The fight was violent and on November 8th the attack of the "Centauro" Division was suspended, from the 15th the retreat began that ended around December 27th when the two columns met near Argirocaster. From that date until the middle of January the Regiment was dismembered, the 2nd Battalion L Tanks of Lieutenant Colonel Pannaciulli was sent to Himara, where on Christmas day an ammunition depot exploded, the IV Battalion of Lieutenant Colonel Zappalà reached the area of Logorath, the 1st Battalion under the command of the Major Congedo was deployed in the Voiussa valley north of Tepeleni, while the III Battalion was transferred to the Devoli valley, outside the dependencies of the 31st Regiment. Meanwhile, on November 12th, coming from Bari, where it had embarked on the 11th, the IV Medium Tank Battalion of the 32nd Carristi Regiment of the "Ariete" Division landed in Durazzo, which was placed first under the direct control of the Supercommando of Albania, then of an Army Corp and finally employed by the 31st Carristi Regiment. On November 20th began the shift towards the front line and from the early days of December began a tiring and grueling series of displacements of platoons or companies to the places where the pressure of the Greeks was stronger, in some cases the tanks were sent to crossings mountains of over 2,000 meters, where their usefulness was absolutely nothing, but

on the other hand the transfers wore engines, mechanical organs, brakes and often the armored vehicles risked falling into the deep cliffs.

In early January 1941 the two Companies of the IV Medium Tank Battalion met to be moved to the Klisura hold, a point of strategic importance for the Italian defense and a starting point for offensive bets that could lighten the pressure on the Golico peaks. In collaboration with the L tanks of the II Battalion, on 27th January, after reconnaissance carried out in the previous days by the commander of the 1st Company Lieutenant Passalacqua, in the morning the Platoon of Lieutenant Panetta set off for the attack which, having seen the bridge over the Desnizes interrupted and the impossibility of fording the river, it returned to the starting base with the carts damaged, but in the afternoon, at the strict command of the Army Command, a second platoon, under the command of Lieutenant Sategna, retried the attack. As already verified by Lieutenant Panetta, it was impossible to cross the stream, but the attack took place and ended with the annihilation of the Platoon, with three tanks destroyed and the only one survived tank managed to return with dead and wounded. The Lieutenant Passalacqua, in the courageous attempt to find and recover survivors, left followed by Lieutenant Panetta's wagon, but the armored vehicles of the two officers, as soon as they arrived on the site where the wreckage of the Sategna platoon lay, were themselves centered by the salvation of dozens of anti-tank and field guns that the Greeks had piled over the ford. The tank of Lieutenant Passalacqua was able to return to the starting base, but subsequently all the members of the crew perished, while the second tank stopped before arriving safely and the crew had to abandon the vehicle, putting themselves on foot until the lines held by the Bersaglieri. For the action conducted on Lieutenant Passalacqua, the Gold Medal for Military Valor will be awarded. As a result of the reckless use of tanks, in this action the IV Battalion lost 7 tanks, two officers and fifteen men, a heavy budget for a null result, although already discounted at the start. From that date the light and medium tanks, under the valid and decisive command of Colonel De Lorenzis, commander of the 31st Regiment and manager of the Voiussa sector, began a continuous series of small, modest but profitable actions, made of shelling and strafing towards the Greek lines and rapid detachments, which caused a state of continuous alertness in the enemy. In February, during these actions, two more M13/40s were lost in the Zagorias hold.

In mid-March a Platoon of medium tanks was sent to support the Arditi in the conquest of Quota 731, the sacred quota of Monastir, but also this action resulted in a failure with the loss of 4 tanks, three destroyed by the enemy and one finished off road. Meanwhile the corvè of the small L3 tanks continued, incessantly playing the role of mobile machine guns, transporting food, ammunition, mail and runners. Between 23rd and 24th March the Regiment, composed of the remains of the three Light Tanks Battalions and the IV Tanks Battalion, moved near Tirana, where they spent a week dedicated to reorganization and rest, after five long months of continuous activity. Following the dripping of vehicles immediately in the preceding months, on March 24th the IV Battalion could only have 18 efficient M13/40 tanks. The regimental workshop worked at full speed to get the vehicles up and running, but if at the end of the rest period the three L Battalions were all in full working order, the M Tanks Battalion had to proceed with the dismantling of the most battered tanks in order to maintain only 18 tanks able to fight.

Thanks to the arrival from Italy of two Battalions of complements it was possible to flesh out the most tried-and-tested units, while the rest of the newcomers went to form two Battalions of "Carristi Appiedati", which would then well behave during the campaign against Yugoslavia.

Invasion of Yugoslavia

On March 25th, 1941, Prime Minister Cvetkovic signed the adhesion pact of Yugoslavia to the Triple Allianc between Italy, Germany and Japan and this marked the end of the country. Only 36 hours later, following this adhesion, a part of the Yugoslav Armed Forces (the Belgrade Air Force and Garrison) carried out a rapid coup d'état, which had overthrown the neutral and pro-Axis government, proclaiming the young Peter II king of Yugoslavia. On 27th March, the new government disavowed its accession to the Tripartite Pact and on 5th April signed a non-aggression pact with Russia. As a result of this sudden change in alliances, the Royal Army immediately sent numerous Divisions both to the border with Italy and to the one with Albania. In fact, the Yugoslav Army was amassing a powerful army of four Quaternary Divisions on the borders with Albania, starting offensive bets aimed at occupying substantial portions of Albanian territory, while on the border with Italy the situation was more peaceful. Adolf Hitler decided to punish the "unfaithful" ally and on the morning of 6th April 1941 the "Unternehemen 25" operation was launched, which began with the bombing of the capital Belgrade, causing the command structure of the new Yugoslavian government to collapse. German diplomacy immediately pressured to involve the Allied countries, Italy, Bulgaria and Hungary, in this war: on 6th April, Italy began hostilities against Yugoslavia. As for the armored units, the 131st Armored Division "Centauro", which was in Albania, the 133rd Armored Division "Littorio", 3 Fast Divisions and the Motorized Divisions "Pasubio" and "Torino" were alerted. The armored component of the Italian units was equipped exclusively with L3 light tanks, a limited number of obsolete L5 tanks (better known as FIAT 3000) and very few M13/40 tanks.

On the Albanian front the 31st Carristi Regiment was immediately sent to Scutari, where on 4th April the I, II and IV L Tanks Battalions and the IV M Tanks arrived, while the III L Tank Battalion remained on the Greek front. In the zone, the "Centauro" Division reunited after many months, since in addition to the 31st Carri Regiment, the 1st Bersaglieri Regiment was present, which had taken the place of the 5th, on two Battalions, one of Cyclists and one Motorbikers Company, the 19th Regiment "Cavalleggeri Guide", the XXII Bersaglieri Motorbikers Battalion, the 131st Engineers Company and the 131rd Artillery Regiment. The units were busy constructing a defensive line that, despite being very thin, still guaranteed a valid barrier to the Yugoslav advance. In addition, the area in front, which goes from Lake Scutari to the first mountainous offshoots of Kosovo, was flat and therefore lent itself finally to the mass use of tanks. Even the two large beds of the rivers Proni Banush and Proni That were almost dry, with the presence of sparse woods and modest inhabited areas: it was just the right terrain to move tank's formations to mass! The front, however, remained defended by a few troops, who failed to cover the entire defensive line, which was so frequently infiltrated by Yugoslav units among the strongholds: in the night between 7th and 8th April a massive frontal attack and on the back of the lines of defense, carried out with a landing from the lake of a strong opposing nucleus, was crushed by the tanks on foot, with the capture of many prisoners. In anticipation of further attacks, the command of the 31st Regiment ordered that the remaining forces of the IV Medium Tank Battalion would pass into the employ of the Light Tank Battalions, so the 1st Company under Lieutenant Panetta came under the command of the 4th Battalion L of Lieutenant Colonel Zappalà, while the 2nd Company of the Lieutenant Chamber went into the employ of the 1st Battalion L Tanks of the Major Congedo. It should be remembered that, although the Carri M Battalion had absorbed the Command Company, the two Companies could dispose of no more than only 8/9 tanks M 13/40. Until 13th April there was a continuous attempt by the Yugoslav side to break through or circumvent the Italian defensive line, with a succession of interventions by the 31st that, in mixed groups of tanks L and M, crushed all attempts by capturing hundreds of prisoners. The Yugoslavs settled on the bank of the Proni That, beginning negotiations to reach the armistice and surrender, but while they sent parliamentarians to the command of the "Centaur" to negotiate, at the same time they arranged to place dozens of anti-tank guns on the bank of the stream. The negotiations were broken, at 4:30 pm on April 15th, the strict order to move forward, pass Proni That and head towards Ivanaj arrived at the Command of the 31st Regiment. Colonel De Lorenzis ordered the I and IV Battalion L Tanks for the attack, with the support of the platoons of M 13/40, holding the II L Tanks Battalion as a reserve and ordered the attack at 6 pm. Everything seemed to be going well but , arrived about two hundred meters from the Proni That, the furious reaction of the Yugoslavs was unleashed, which with dozens of machine guns and anti-tank guns invested the mass of the tanks hitting them repeatedly. It was a dramatic moment as the precise fire of the enemy opened fearful gaps between the tankers rows but, the timely intervention of Lieutenant Colonel Zappalà who, regardless of the risk of the bridge being undermined, ordered the crossing of the road bridge to the tanks of the 1st Battalion, solved the critical situation that had arisen, by bypassing and taking the Yugoslav positions, which also had to face the tanks that had managed to ford the stream and were now investing the Yugoslavian cannon line. The enemy took to flight, but the victory had required a high toll of blood, in the last battle on Albanian soil 11 L tanks were destroyed and 5 severely damaged, as well as 3 M13/40 tanks destroyed and another damaged. From the 16th the advance in Montenegro continued, which ended along the road from Ragusa to Trebinje, when, meeting the avant-gardes of the "Littorio", the Yugoslav campaign of the 31st Tank Regiment ended. On April 23rd the march back to Albania began, on the 25th the Regiment paraded in Scutari at the presence of the authorities, on the 26th it reached Durazzo, on the 27th Fieri, on the 28th Tepeleni and finally on the 29th it arrived at Giorguzzati (south of Gjirokaster) , where the news finally arrived that the campaign was over. The 31st Regiment at Giorguzzati was joined by the 3rd L Tanks Battalion, detached for the entire campaign at the 9th Army, and by all the units scattered in Albania, including the Complementary Battalions, thus beginning a reorganization of the somewhat battered vehicles. When in the middle of May the 31st reached Durazzo, the four L Tanks Battalions were completed in means and personnel, while the IV Medium Tanks, despite the recovery of the vehicles left on the mountains on the border with Greece, did not align more than fourteen tanks. Around May 20th, convoys started to leave for Italy, and the 31st Regiment finally returned to its settlements at the mouth of the Tagliamento, where the Battalions were reequipped with M tanks.

The 1st Border Guards Tank Company (G.a.F.), from its garrison in Scutari, was transferred to the Tarabosch - Bojana sector and included in the 3rd Battalion G.a.F., in defense of the anti-tank barrier of Kurt Alai on the Scutari - Antivari road. After successfully facing a Yugoslav attack on April 11th, the Company remained stationary even when, on the 15th, Italian troops attacked and began their advance towards Montenegro. The 1st Border Guards Tank Company then returned to Scutari performing defense functions.

On the Italian border, at the beginning of April the "Littorio" Armored Division, with the 33rd Tank Regiment on three Light Tanks Battalions with 117 L tanks, reached the Karst plateau, forming a semicircle around Trieste, assuming a purely defensive array. After a few days, after waiting for orders from Rome, on April 10th, General Ambrosio issued the order of movement. The advance developed on two main directions penetrating from Postumia, towards Ljubljana and towards Zagreb and the Dalmatian coast. Towards Zagreb the "Littorio" moved, while towards Ljubljana the "Eugenio di Savoia" Division. The "Littorio", with the 33rd Tank Regiment in the lead, converged on Fiume and at 22:00 began its advance along the Dalmatian coast. The advance continued towards Karlovac, where it met the German avant-gardes and, consequently, the Division deviated towards the south, reaching Ogulin, later Otocac and Gospic, to finally arrive at Grapac. After a few brief skirmishes with Yugoslav departments at the Mostar airfield, the race continued to Montenegro. On 17th April in Trebinje a meeting took place with the units of the "Centauro" Division from Albania. Approximately 1,000 km were traveled, in what can be defined as a race against time rather than a war action, given that the Yugoslav army did not oppose the slightest resistance to the units of the Division. After a brief stay in Mostar, the "Littorio" in May returned to Italy, where its Battalions were reequipped with M. The 1st Celere Division "Eugenio di Savoia", deployed from the beginning of March in the Montespino - Rifembergo - San Daniele del Carso - Duttogliano - Tomadio - Comeno area, was initially not used, remaining firm on its positions. On 11th April a Fast Group was established with the aim of occupying Ljubljana. The "San Giusto" Light Tanks Group, with 61 L tanks, was included in the Fast Grou. At 4:00 pm the Group crossed the border at Kalce and, proceeding at a fast pace on the Logatec - Ljubljana rolling stock, its vanguard, of which it was part of the 1st L Tanks Squadron, entered the Slovenian capital without encountering resistance at 6.30pm. On April 13th, Easter Day, the Fast Group, with the Tanks Group "San Giusto" always in the vanguard, received the order to continue south, with the aim of dispersing the remaining efficient formations of the Yugoslav army. Passing through Toplice - Vrbovsko - Petrovo Selo - Gornji Lapac - Zemanya Velo - Gracac - Gospic, the "San Giusto" did not support any fighting, but carried out only a few roundups. On 27th April the Fast Group was dissolved, the Group "San Giusto" returned to the dependencies of the 1st Fast Division and began the transfer, made difficult by the abundant snowfall, towards Dugaresa, south-west of Karlovac, where it will be housed. The 1st Fast Division "Eugenio di Savoia" remained displaced in Yugoslavia until the armistice, involved with all its departments in the fierce guerrilla war unleashed a few months after the official end of hostilities.

The 2nd Fast Division "Emanuele Filiberto Testa di Ferro" (E.F.T.F.) participated with its units in the invasion of Yugoslavia, reaching Delnice, Ogulin and finally Korenica. In the 2nd Fast Division was present the II L Tanks Group "San Marco", equipped with 61 light tanks. Once the hostilities ended, the Tank Group "San Marco", with about 30 tanks, took part in some mopping up operations in Croatia and Bosnia, but at the end of July 1941 it returned to Italy.

Also the 3rd Fast Division "Prince Amedeo Duca d'Aosta" (P.A.D.A.) contributed with its units to the invasion of Yugoslavia. Displaced on the Italian-Yugoslav border, on 13th April it entered enemy territory, reaching in the following days Jelenje, Kubjak, Cakovac and Slunj. On 20th April the departments occupied Rakovica, Drazik Grad, Bihac and 22th Trogir, Split and Karlovac. In Split the Division remained committed until May 31st in mopping up operations, then returned to Italy. In the 3rd Fast Division there was the 3rd L Tanks Group "San Giorgio", with 61 tanks L.

The Zara Mechanized Company also took part in the operations against Yugoslavia. This Company had been in the Dalmatian city since 1935 and it was equipped with L and FIAT 3000 tanks and a pair of Lancia 1ZM armored cars. Together with the Bersaglieri of the IX Battalion, it occupied Bencovac and Knin, then progressing up to Sibenik and Spalato.

▼ L3 tanks are embarked in the port of Brindisi to be sent to Albania

▲ A CV35 of the 2nd Bersaglieri Regiment lands in the port of Durres during the first phases of the occupation of Albania in 1939 (Benvenuti - Colonna)

▲ Italian units, supported by armored vehicles, advance inside Durres without encountering any resistance (Benvenuti - Colonna)

▼ A platoon of L3 tanks parked in Durres, waiting to resume the advance towards the Albanian capital Tirana, including one with a trailer (Benvenuti - Colonna)

▲ A small contingent of tanks advances in the narrow main street of a village in Albania, among the indifference of the inhabitants (Crippa)

▲ Entrance of the first Italian tanks in Tirana (Benvenuti - Colonna)

▲ With the entry of Italian troops to Tirana, the short campaign of Albania was concluded (Benvenuti - Colonna)
▼ To celebrate the very rapid Albanian campaign, a parade was organized in Durres of the units that had taken part in the invasion. In this image the tanks of the Armored Company of the 2nd Bersaglieri Regiment (Benvenuti - Colonna)

▲ A Platoon of Armored Companies of the 31st Tanks Infantry Regiment of the "Centauro" Division parades, equipped with L3 and L3 Flamethrowers (Benvenuti - Colonna)
▼ M13/40 tank of the IV Medium Tank Battalion of the 32nd Tanks Regiment of the "Aries" Division in Albania, ready to cross the border with Greece in November 1940

▲ A L3 tank Flame thrower in action on the Greek front (Benvenuti - Colonna)

▼ CV33 in Voiussa Valley heavily masked with fronds (Benvenuti - Colonna)

▲ Emblematic image of the unfortunate Greek campaign: a CV35 reduced badly by enemy fire. The crew removed the machine guns before leaving the tank (Benvenuti - Colonna)

▼ A platoon of L3 Flamethrowers advances on a dusty road during the Greek Campaign: they are all deprived of the trailer with the flammable liquid (Benvenuti - Colonna)

▲ Motorcycle divisions of the Regio Esercito cross the Sussak bridge in Rijeka, which marked the border between Italy and the Kingdom of Yugoslavia at 17.00 on 11th April 1941, after the unconditional surrender of the Yugoslav garrison had been dealt with in the Office of Police station near the bridge (Arena)

▼ CV35 tanks enter the populous Croatian district of Sussak aboard a forklift truck, pulled by trucks (Arena)

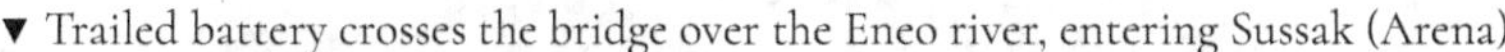

▲ A L3/35 Flamethrower tank with its trailer containing the flammable liquid (Arena)

▼ Trailed battery crosses the bridge over the Eneo river, entering Sussak (Arena)

▲ The entry of Italian troops to Sussak (Cronache di Guerra)

▲ M13/40 tank of the 33rd Battalion of the "Littorio" Division while facing the ascent of the current Ulica Franje Račkoga to Sussak (Cronache di Guerra)
▼ A formation of tanks L3 and M13 of the "Littorio" Division while entering Sussak (Benvenuti - Colonna)

▲ Italian L3/35 tanks on the border line with Greece are preparing to enter enemy territory (Arena)

▼ L3/35 tanks of the "Centauro" Division parked on the road to Giannina during the invasion of Yugoslav territory (Benvenuti - Colonna)

▲ A L3/35, loaded to an incredible extent with provisions, is about to cross a bridge in Yugoslav territory (Benvenuti - Colonna)

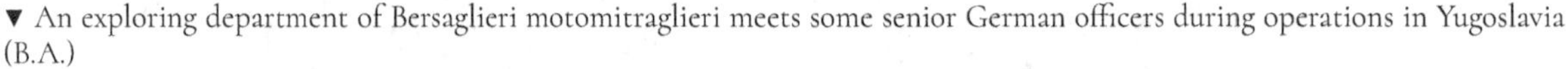

▲ A CV35 of the "Centaur" armed with Breda machine guns. The armored vehicle is completely covered by the dust raised during the march, so as to make the color of the armor unrecognizable

▼ An exploring department of Bersaglieri motomitraglieri meets some senior German officers during operations in Yugoslavia (B.A.)

▲ Column of light tanks advances in Dalmatian territory during the first phases of occupation of Yugoslavia. It is interesting to use the tricolor on the leading half, to identify the nationality of the unit

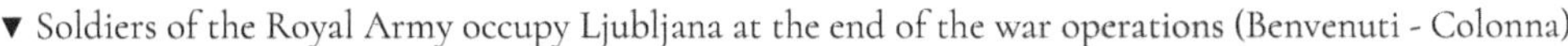

▼ Soldiers of the Royal Army occupy Ljubljana at the end of the war operations (Benvenuti - Colonna)

▲ A Division of Bersaglieri enters the historical center of Dubrovnik, between two wings of perplexed inhabitants of the city

▲ Field Marshal Von List and General Ambrosio photographed after the signing of the surrender of the Yugoslav Armed Forces in Belgrade (Arena)

▼ Part of the war booty captured from the Yugoslav royal army: a large part of the armament is made up of French-made material (Arena)

THE ITALIAN OCCUPATION

Once the hostilities ended, with the unconditional surrender of Yugoslavia signed on April 17th and the armistice with Greece requested on the 29th, the tank's units began their return to Italy. In Yugoslavia and Albania armored units were no longer present in June, except for the 1st Frontier Tank Company, equipped with FIAT 3000 of little or no use. The unconditional surrender of Yugoslavia led to the annexation of parts of Slovenia and Kosovo, of Dalmatia to Split, including almost all the islands, part of Croatia and Montenegro, the latter officially constituted as an autonomous state. The war ended on paper in mid-April, but under the ashes of the surrender the spirit of the rebellion brooded, fomented by the Yugoslav military, defeated but left free and, in the overwhelming majority, even armed, by the communists and the struggles between the various ethnic groups. The Royal Army, unprepared and not trained to face the partisan's guerrilla, had to transfer hundreds of thousands of men and hundreds of vehicles to control the immense occupied territory, suffering thousands of losses. From July 1941 to September 8th, 1943, it was a continuous alternation of gunfights, raids, ambushes, reprisals and many were the tanks units involved. Equipped with armaments abandoned by the Yugoslav army now in disarray, the civilian populations gave rise to a partisan movement that forced the Italian Army to continue operations of control of the territory and of repression: attacks on isolated soldiers, on garrisons, on police cars and sabotage was the order of the day, but only on 1st March 1942 a circular was issued governing counter-insurgency operations and the use of armored vehicles in this difficult context. In particular, with regard to the safety of columns of vehicles, it was suggested that the means that had to open and close the columns were armored, at least with waste materials, and armed with machine guns, in order to open fire quickly in the event of hostile acts. In the same circular the units present in Balcania were exhorted to prepare trucks with "field" protections, with plates or even with sandbags, waiting for mass-produced vehicles. The cars produced "out of series" were of the most different types, from those made in an extremely artisanal manner and in very limited numbers, if not unique, to more elaborate vehicles, initially however with open top, a detail that exposed the occupants of the vehicles to the launch of hand grenades. To overcome this drawback, body protection systems were devised with bomb nets or armor plates positioned in the upper part. In particular, French war prey trucks were used for these productions: trench shields were secured on the three sides of the caisson, on which slits were made, in varying numbers, which allowed the crew to open fire and remain sheltered. The first specimens of these protected trucks were without protections for the cabin and for the fuel tanks, extremely vulnerable points; later were also made for these parts of the vehicles with normal sheets. In later times the Protected AS37s arrived in the Balkans, which were not suitable for use on the African front for which they had been designed, and the most popular FIAT 665 NM "Scudato".

It is impossible to list all the actions in which the armored vehicles were used, also because in almost all cases they were activities carried out at platoon level or even just wagon sections. We will however try to give a picture as complete as possible of their employment during the anti-partisan struggle.

On 13th July 1941 the rebellion in Montenegro exploded unexpectedly. The garrison troops were put in serious difficulty: communications were interrupted, roads made dangerous or impassable, the largest garrisons isolated, and the small ones overwhelmed. The "Messina" Division was established in Montenegro, supported by a Public Safety Motorcyclist Battalion, Carabinieri departments and the II and VI Guardia di Finanza Battalion. The support of the 1st Frontier Tanks Company was immediately requested, equipped only with old L5 carts, which, together with the II Battalion of the Guardia di Finanza, began the transfer to Podgorica. The transfer of the Company had to be carried out on tracks, due to the absence of chariot carts, so the 8 tanks arrived in Podgorica only on April 15th, in practice to travel the 70 km of the journey they took over 18 hours!! Arriving at its destination, the 1st Company was ordered to move to Cettigne, the capital of Montenegro, but, given the conditions of the tanks, the order was canceled, and the ward remained in Podgorica to put the end of life vehicles into gear. The 1st Frontier Tanks Company remained therefore until the date of the Armistice stationed in Podgorica, with tasks of mobile defense and from June 1942 entered the staff of the 3rd L Tanks Battalion of the 31st Tanker Infantry Regiment of the "Centaur" Division.

On July 25th, 1941, the Command, I and II L Tanks Battalions of the 31st Regiment were transferred to Dalmatia with the utmost urgency to counter the revolt that also took place in Croatia. During the transfer, along the Ogulin - Gospic - Knin - Spalato railway line, the convoy carrying the Command Company suffered an attack, caused by the tampering of the tracks, with the derailment of most of the wagons and the loss of many vehicles. Once the railway line was restored, the convoys arrived at their destination. The Command Company and an L Tank Battalion remained in Split, while the other L Tank Battalion was posted to Knin. Work then began in support of infantry units involved in raids or patrols. At the end of August, the Regimental Command Company and the L Tank Battalion from Spalato were transferred to Sibenik. On September 11th, the 31st Regimental Command Company began re-entry into Italy, to return to the "Centaur" Division, engaged in training the new Battalions with armored tanks. The two L Tank Battalions became autonomous and were engaged until the end of September in occupied Dalmatia. In the month of July, the III Battalion of the 31st was also sent to Montenegro, which deployed the 6th Company to Niksic, the 5th to Cettigne, the Command, the Company Command and Services, the workshop and the 4th Company in Podgorica. The 1st Frontier Tank Company was also attached to the III Battalion and, subsequently, a Platoon of armored car coming from the XL Battalion Bersaglieri. Having taken note of the serious situation that had arisen with the recurrence of the Tito's guerrilla warfare, the Supreme Command decided to establish Battalions and Autonomous L Tanks Companies, also flamethrowers, to be sent to Dalmatia and Montenegro. These Battalions and Companies had to be used as mobile reinforcement units, in the operational dependencies of the Divisions spread over the territory. Rarely, however, they were employed at the Company level, most of the time they operated as platoons, or even sections, in mopping up operations, at checkpoints, in garrison activity, as escort to convoys, frustrating what was to be their main task, the war of movement and breaking the front. The losses of both men and means were remarkable. Thus, two L Flamethrowers Battalions were sent to the occupied territories, consisting of the 4th Regiment's depot and employed in Dalmatia and Montenegro. The II Battalion Carriages L Flame thrower operated in reduced ranks, with 16 carts. The II L Flamethrowers Autonomous Company was also set up, again with L Flamethrowers tanks, which operated from March 1942 in Slovenia and Dalmatia, while further autonomous Flamethrowers were established and assigned directly to Infantry departments. Instead, the Zara Mechanized Company operated until the date of the Armistice in the area of Mostar and Ragusa. The III L Tank Battalion of the 31st Regiment participated with the 6th Company in a vast operation of control of the territory on the Montenegrin border at the beginning of August 1942. On some occasions individual platoons were posted to garrisons or for round-ups in support of the "Hunters of the Alps". In the fall Compagnie came back to their seats, preparing for the winter. Because of heavy snowfall, the intense cold that chilled the roads and the partisans who controlled the access roads, Niksic remained isolated for long months, supplied only by air. During this period the L tanks were used at checkpoints and to counter the partisan's exploratory episodes. Finally, in March 1942 the siege ended.

The spring and summer of 1942 for the III Battalion wards passed quite quietly, without particular clashes and noteworthy with the partisans: the disengaged activities were mainly convoy stocks, support for departments engaged in counter-insurgency operations, vehicle maintenance. However, in the first months of 1943 the guerrilla warfare intensified. On May 1st a column, composed of a 47th Regiment Infantry Battalion, a Black Shirts Infantry and an Artillery Battery, escorted by two Platoons of the 6th Company, engaged in an operation to control the territory along the Niksic line - Gorniopolie - Javorach - Savnick, fell into an ambush that caused numerous casualties. The 6th Company lost 3 tanks, complained 2 dead, 2 wounded and 2 prisoners, fortunately released following an exchange of prisoners, other tanks were abandoned after being sabotaged (in a book published in the post-war period in Yugoslavia, the loss is mentioned of 7 Italian tanks). All the units of the column had to return to Niksic, threatened again with siege. In early August, the 6th Company left Niksic, where it had worked for almost two years, and it was reunited with the rest of the Battalion in Podgorica. He had about 40 L tanks out of the 61 in the organic tables.

The I Tank Group "San Giusto" at the end of July 1941 moved to Karlovac, in August its 1st Squadron operated from Ogulin with the "Alessandria" Regiment, until November, participating in a round-up cycle that lasted from 9th to 25th October. The 3rd Squadron was transferred to Topusko, remaining in the area until April 1942. At the end of December, the partisans besieged the town of Korenica, in Lika, where a reinforced Battalion of the 1st Regiment of the Division "Re" was presided over. In the relief operations, aimed at unblocking the siege, the 4th Squadron of the "San Giusto" was engaged, which moved to Plase. Two columns were prepared that were to join up with Bjelo Polje and then continue on Korenica: in the two columns there were vehicles of the 2nd and 4th Squadron of the Group. A column was immediately stopped by the snow blocking the roads, while the second one was stopped by the strong resistance opposed by the partisans, which caused serious losses. The "San Giusto" Group, during the operations, suffered the loss of 3 tankers and wounded 4 other soldiers, the lost tanks were 2, one of which was captured by the Yugoslavs. The release of Korenica was suspended and resumed only in March 1942, when the resistance of the partisans was overcome and the 2nd Squadron of the "San Giusto", together with the tanks of a Flamethrowers Company, it was among the first to enter the liberated town. In April 1942 the 4th Squadron was still employed by the "Re" Division in anti-partisan actions, while in July the 1st Squadron operated under the supervision of the V Border Guard Group in the border area between Italy and Croatia. The 3rd Squadron moved to Vrbovsko, employed by the "Lombardia" Division, where it participated in operations with the Tactical Group Ferroni, to return to Karlovac in late August. In October, the "1st Celere", "Lombardia" and "Cacciatori delle Alpi" Divisions began a cycle of anti-partisan operations in the area around Karlovac, during which the 2nd, 3rd and 4th Squadron were involved. On 17th October the wagons of the 3rd Squadron were involved in what was the last charge of the Italian Cavalry: the position of "Poloj", in which they participated together with the troopers of the "Cavalleggeri di Alessandria" Regiment, and an L tank came captured by the partisans. In November 1942 the 2nd Squadron was deployed to Jastrebarsko. At the end of November, many Italian units withdrew from many areas of the interior of Croatia, concentrating on the defense of strategically more important areas. The "1st Celere" Division left the Karlovac area and moved to the Dalmatian coast, with the command in Sibenik, but the "San Giusto" Group, due to the slow transfer due to various causes, reached Sibenik, where the Command was deployed, only on December 20th. Squadrons were deployed to various units: the 1st Squadron in Sibenik, the 2nd in Split, the 3rd in Knin and the 4th in Benkovac. In mid-January the 1st Squadron was also transferred to Knin, before moving to Split in February and in early March the 3rd Squadron moved to Sinj. From the middle of January to the beginning of March the Operation "Weiss" took place, a vast intervention with the aim of eliminating the partisans from the tar zone, the Karlovac - Ogulin - Knin railway and the Glina - Bosanski Novi - Sanski Most - Kljuc road, attended by German, Italian and Croatian departments. The San Giusto Group also participated in operations with the 4th Squadron and perhaps also with other departments. Towards the end of April the 3rd Squadron moved to Fiume, at the disposal of the "Re" Division, participating in the operations for the reconquest of the Melnice saddle, the Vratnik pass and the Zuta Lokva basin. In May the I L Tanks "San Giusto" Group was equipped with 51 L tanks, compared to the 61 provided by the organic tables. Between the end of May and August, the "San Giusto" Group, following the orders for the transfer of the 1st Celere Division to the northern part of the Dalmatian coast, placed the Command and its Squadrons in the Fiume / Sussak area, apart from the 4th Squadron which remained in the Knin area. On the date of the armistice, the I L Tanks "San Giusto" Group was thus dislocated:

- Command, Command Squadron e workshop in Sussak

- 1st Squadron in Ogulin and Delnice

- 2nd Squadron in Sussak and Crikvenica

- 3rd Squadron in Fiume, Karlobag and Vratnik

- 4st Squadron in Kristanje and Perkovic.

The news of the armistice signature reached them there.

The II Carri L Group "San Marco" in April 1942 participated in the "Trio Operation" which, despite the efforts made and the forces involved, did not reach the desired outcome.

▲ A section of three AB41 armored cars escorting a column of the Royal Army in Dalmatia in 1942 (B.A.)

▼ During the Second World War the Italian Royal Army still employed some aliquots of the old FIAT 3000 tanks. In the photo one of these tanks, in charge of a Border Guard unit in the Balkans in 1941

▲ L3 light tanks during an anti-partisans operation in Croatia (Benvenuti - Colonna)

▼ Italian-German military ceremony at the headquarters of the XXIII Army Corps in Trieste in 1942 (Arena)

▲ Light Tank L3/35 of the IV Company of the 31st Tanks Regiment in a Dalmatian village

▲ A M13/40 tank at the ford of a stream in Albania (Arena)

▼ Group of riflemen of the 85th Battalion "M" Apuania of M.VS.N. near Karlovac (Croatia) before an action in front of a fully camouflaged protected AS37 (Cataldi)

▲ This image is emblematic of the transport situation in the occupied Balkans: it was necessary to have a supply of armored vehicles (in this case an Autoprotetto AS37 and an AB41) to be able to move safely, due to the high risk of ambushes (Arena)

▲ An armored truck of the 2nd Army in a Slovenian village. The resurgence of the partisan guerrilla warfare in the Balkans found the Royal Army unprepared, which had to equip itself with armored trucks, even in the traditional way, to protect the troops during their journeys (Arena)

▼ Even the senior officers of the Regio Esercito used artisanal armored vehicles for their own transfers, so as to minimize the risks associated with possible partisan attacks (Arena)

▲ This SPA CL39 small truck of the 18th Mortar Battalion of the "Messina" Division, photographed in Cattaro on 20th September 1942, received a makeshift protection, necessary to defend the occupants of the vehicle

▲ An Italian armored truck (probably a Bianchi Mediolanum) in Gerovu in 1942

▼ A group of legionaries of M.V.S.N. aboard a French ADR truck during a roundup in a Yugoslav village in 1943

▲ Greek Militia - Orthodox of the Anti-Communist Voluntary Militia aboard an armored AS37 of the Royal Army in 1943 (Arena)

▼ FIAT 3000 Model 21 Tank in Montenegro. Note the white coloring of the turret hat, useful for aerial identification of friendly vehicles (Benvenuti - Colonna)

▲ Another obsolete FIAT 3000 model 21 (probably of G.A.F.) on the inaccessible Balkan land in 1941 (Benvenuti - Colonna)

▼ A train loaded with FIAT 665NM armored trucks of fresh production as soon as they arrived in the Balkans

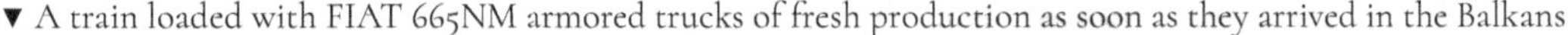

▲ The 31st Tanks Regiment deployed in Piazza Scanderberg in Tirana in the spring of 1940 on the occasion of the visit of Marshal De Bono (Ratti)

▼ Scutari, 25th April 1941: the 31st Regiment parades at the end of the short campaign against Yugoslavia (Ratti)

▲ Opening ceremony of the war cemetery of the 31st Carristi Regiment in Giorguzzati, Albania (Ratti)

▼ L tanks, vehicles and baggage in Albania (Ratti)

▲ Officers of the III L Tanks Battalion of the 31st Regiment in Albania (Ratti)

▼ The M 13/40 tank of the Lieutenant Panetta (Arena)

▲ Tankers of the III Battalion of 31st Regiment in front of a tankette (Ratti)

▼ Tank wardens of the 6th Company intent on maintaining an L tank (Ratti)

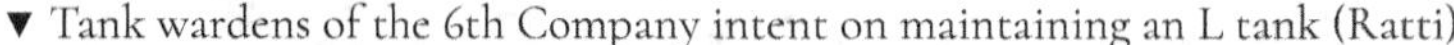

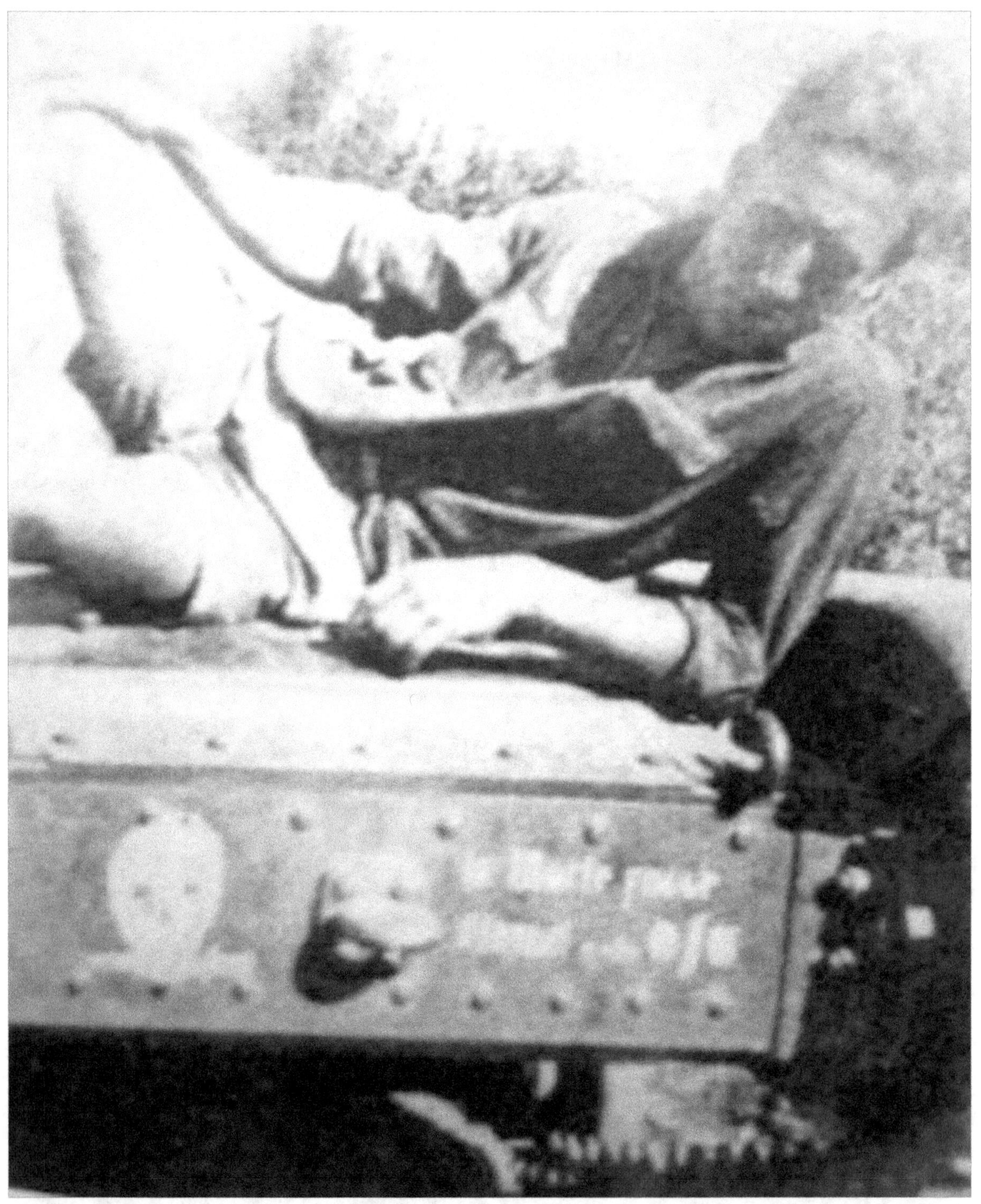

▲ Curious foreground of an L tankette of the 31st Tanks Regiment in the Premeti area: on the front of the small tank, note the inscription "Death flees before those who dare" and the skull that refers to the iconography dear to the Arditi (Ratti)

▲ Cart L 3 of the 6th Company of the 3rd Tank Battalion at Niksic (Ratti)

▼ A CV33 from the 6th Company challenges the snow during the winter of 1942 at Niksic (Ratti)

▲ The 2nd Platoon of the 6th Company III L Tanks Battalion L arked during a counter guerrilla operation in Montenegro in the summer of 1942 (Ratti)

▼ L tankette of the commander of the 3rd Platoon of the 6th Company of the III L Tanks Battalion of the 31st Regiment: the mimetic in patches is very clearly visible (Ratti)

▲ The 6th Company of the III L Tanks Battalion in Niksic. On the first tank Captain Ripandelli, commander of the Company (Ratti)

▼ Recovery of a lost tankette during an action against the Tito's guerrillas in Montenegro in the summer of 1943 (Ratti)

▲ Blessing of the L6s of the 19th "Guide" Regiment in Tirana in 1943 (Benvenuti - Colonna)

▼ Deployment of the 19th "Cavalleggeri Guide" Regiment in Tirana in 1943 (Benvenuti - Colonna)

▲ Another image of the same ceremony. A strong rate of the L6/40s was destined to the Cavalry units deployed in the Balkans (Crippa)

▼ Exercise of the "Cavalleggeri Guide" in Tirana (Benvenuti - Colonna)

▲ Another image of the same tank L6/40 of the 19th "Guide" Regiment (Benvenuti - Colonna)

▼ L6/40 tanks of a Cavalry unit (probably "Monferrato Regiment) in Tirana in 1943 (Benvenuti - Colonna)

ARMORED ITALIAN RAILWAY IN THE BALNKANS

During the Second World War, Italy used armed trains and railway artilleries, both of the Royal Navy and of the Railway Engeneers, which had already been part of the Italian defenses during the Great War. At the beginning of 1942 these convoys were progressively transferred to the territories of the former Yugoslavia. Placed under the command of the 2nd Army and operated by personnel of the Genius Engineers, these trains underwent adaptations, useful to face the risks linked to possible partisan attacks: the locomotives were armored and the wagons were equipped with flamethrowers and mortars. The tasks assigned to these trains in the Balkan territory were the escort to the railway convoys and the patrolling of the railroads, often the target of sabotage carried out by the local resistance. In a region, such as the Balkans, lacking an effective road network, trains were the main means of transport also for the Armed Forces and therefore the defense of railways was essential, to avoid sabotage and line interruptions. However, the use of these armed trains did not prove to be an optimal solution for the control of the railway networks, so much so that at the beginning of 1942 studies began for some armored vehicles designed specifically for patrolling the railways, for the protection of the troops of the Railway Engeneers at work and to quickly bring fire protection to railway stations or convoys subjected to enemy attacks.

On January 24th, 1942, the Motor State Office of the General Staff of the Royal Army issued a note with the subject "Armored Car 41 Railway", which was urgently requested to be built of an undefined number of AB 41 modified so that they could also circulate on ordinary gauge railways. The SPA was activated immediately and were transformed into "Autobindo Ferroviarie" both AB40s, with the peculiar turret with Breda 38 twin machine guns, and the more widespread AB41s with the 20 mm machine gun, which, finally, some AB43s, the latter after the Armistice. Before the Armistice, a total of 20 armored cars were built, all registered on 8th May 1942 (but they reached the department they belonged to in several phases, the last in August of the same year). On the 15th of the same month the Autonomous Railway Company was set up, used by the 2nd Group of Railway Engineers Mobilized, organized on Command with Platoon Command and 2 Platoons Armored Cars with 5 machines each. On May 28th, another 10 armored cars were assigned to the Company, so much so that on August 28th the Company was reorganized into 4 Platoons. The railway ABs were located in the territories of the former Yugoslavia, for which they had been specifically designed; the Company was thus distributed throughout the territory:

• Command and a Platoon with reserve functions to Sussak (available to the High Command);

• Half Platoon in Ljubljana and the other half Platoon in Novo Mesto, both available for the XI Army Corps;

• Two Platoons in Ogulin, available to the V Corps;

• A Platoon in Knin.

The intended use was to reinforce the armed escort of the trains used for transporting materials for re-routing and reconnaissance of the lines and patrolling them. Operationally, in addition to performing these tasks, railway armored cars were often used to create armored convoys made up of a Littorina Blindata and an AB, with tasks to protect the railways of Slovenia and Dalmatia. They rendered precious services on the railways in the areas infested by the Tito's partisans, sometimes even being used for the swift transportation of senior officers visiting advanced garrisons in particularly risky areas. The machines that survived the Armistice were used by the German Armed Forces, both on the railway and as normal armored cars.

Also in 1942 the General Staff of the Royal Army decided to adopt a modified, armored "Littorina" on the chassis of the FIAT ALN 56 model, named "Li.Bli. (acronym of Littorina Blindata) model 42 ", armed with 2 modified M13/40 tank turrets, armed with 47/32 cannon, twin with Breda 38 machine gun and, on each side, 2 Breda 38 machine guns on spherical support and one Breda 38 for shooting with strong angles, 2 45 mm mortars in cockpit and 2 Model 40 portable flamethrowers. On 18th August the 1st Littorine Armored Company on Command (Command and Command Squadron) and two Armored Littorine Platoons was established. The Company was employed exclusively in the territories of the former Yugoslavia, carrying out intense work of anti-sabotage surveillance of the railway lines and escorting the convoys, integrating the work of the railway armored cars, acting as Head of the Italian 2nd Army in Sussak. The 8 Littorinas produced of the Model 42 were located in Susa, Novo Mesto, Ogulin, Ljubljana, Lalovac and Spalato, practically, therefore, in the whole Yugoslav territory. The Li.Bli. 1 was seriously damaged in Spalato in October 1942; the Li.Bli. 2 was lost near Ogulin on 12th February 1943: it was derailed by the explosion of a mine placed on the railway station by partisans and could no longer be recovered due to the lack of suitable equipment. The serious accident caused many casualties among crew members, including the Commander of the Littorine Autonomous Company. On March 8th, 1943, the composition of the Autonomous Company Littorine Blindate was modified and the new structure included Commander, Command Platoon and Littorinas; in addition to the rolling stock, 1 car, 3 SPA 38R trucks, 2 motorcycles and 1 bicycle were included in the workforce. Each Littorina had to have a crew composed of 1 junior officer, 2 conductors, 2 gunners, of which 1 non-commissioned officer acting as deputy commander, 2 servants, 6 machine-gunners, 2 mortars, 2 flamethrower operators and 1 radio operator; the conductors were called up to arms, with license of Italian Railways.

After the Armistice also the Li.Bli. survivors suffered the same fate as most of the weapons of the disbanded Regio Esercito, ending up confiscated by German troops; however, two Littorinas continued to be operated, at least until the spring of 1944, by Italian crews. These two Li.Bli. patrolled the Friuli railways, in particular the Gorizia - Piedicolle line (valleys of Isonzo and Baccia) and the Gorizia - Trieste and Gorizia - Udine lines, based on the Gorizia - Montesanto station (now Nova Gorica station in Slovenia). They worked in concert with the "Carlevaris" group, which defended the city of Gorizia and, for the entire spring of 1944, one of the two Li.Bli. placed the the Bersaglieri Volunteer Battalion "Benito Mussolini" in Val Baccia. Meanwhile, Ansaldo had developed a second version of the Littorina Blindata, the so-called

"Model 43", armed with a Breda model 35 20mm caliber machine gun on a candlestick support positioned in the center of the wagon. The production of this second version was carried out for the Germans at the beginning of 1944 (the first specimens entered service in May) and were used intensively by the German Armed Forces in Croatia, Slovenia and Bosnia. In 1942 a limited number of OM 36 lorries was transformed into an armored vehicle for patrolling the narrow-gauge railway lines of the Balkans. This project stemmed from a specific need of the High Command of the Armed Forces of Slovenia and Dalmatia, since an armored vehicle was needed to be used in security service on the railways of 76 cm of Herzegovina. The prototype of the curious armored vehicle was tested on the march of the Val Gardena railway, which had characteristics similar to those in which the Autocarretta Ferroviaria actually operated, giving good proof of itself and officially entered service on 18 December 1942, under the name of Armored Railway "Autocarretta" model 42. The employment on the lines Ragusa - Mostar and Spalato - Sinj by personnel of the Raylway Engineers showed a big limit, especially in relation to the operating conditions in areas infested by the partisans. The armored vehicle, in fact, was not equipped with a double guide and therefore, in the case of sabotage of the railway line or ambush, it was not possible to reverse the direction of travel. Therefore, a solution to this drawback was studied, that is, to proceed, if necessary, to raise the wagon with a hydraulic jack, placed under the center of the vehicle, which thus allowed it to be rotated... by hand, a maneuver that exposed to the enemy fire the crew members. The structure of the vehicle was unfortunately very light and the armament, consisting of 1 Breda 38 machine gun and a Breda submachine gun, was too modest for the conditions in which the lorries operated. An autonomous unit was set up on May 15th, 1943 (Autonomous Wagon Armored Railroad Car Service) on the orders of the General Staff of the Royal Army, consisting of Commander, Command Squadron and Services, 2 Autocarretta's Platoons, with a staff of 1 officer, 2 non-commissioned officers and 56 men of troop. The equipment of the unit was 20 railcars, 1 light truck and 1 bicycle. The vehicles that survived the Armistice were confiscated by the German Armed Forces, who continued to use them on the lines for which they were designed.

▲ Legionaries of the Railway Militia patrol a stopover in Slovenia. The safety of the railway lines in the Balkans required a constant and onerous commitment to the Italian Armed Forces: the train represented the best means of transport and communication in the inaccessible Yugoslav territory and for this reason the railway lines were very often the target of partisan attacks (Arena)

▲ We are near a railway station in the Balkans and an AB40 Ferroviaria is parked, surrounded by soldiers of the Royal Army. The men of the armored car are easily identifiable, as they wear the uniform of the armored units (Crippa)

▲ Often the railway armored cars traveled in convoys formed by two cars, as in this photograph: the vehicles are coupled by coupling the engines. The crew in this case is strangely formed by soldiers of the Railway Militia (Crippa)

▼ Another AB41 Railway stationed near a station in the territories of the former Yugoslavia. The vehicles of this production lot were all painted in a monochromatic yellow (Crippa)

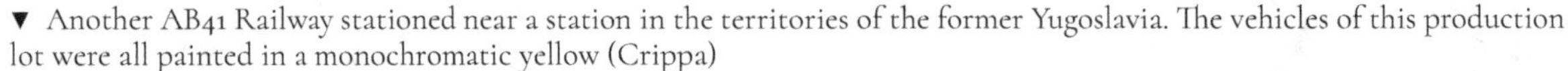

▲ A Li.Bli. Model 42 with its crew in the Balkans; note the position of the license plate on the left side of the locomotive (Arena)

▼ Littorina Li.Bli. Model 42 parked on the railway between Split and Knin in 1942; photography allows us to appreciate the particular camouflage color (Crippa)

▲ Convoy formed by an AB41 and a Littorina Blindata brings aid near Ogulin on 12th February 1943 to Li.Bli. derailed because of a mine placed on the railway site, an accident that cost the life of the Commander of the "1st Autonomous Littorine Company" (Arena)

▼ On the Li.Bli. Model 43, named by the Germans "Panzertriebwagen Typ 62", a Breda 20 mm was installed on a candlestick support in the center of the car (Arena)

▲ One of the two Li.Bli. who patrolled the Gorizia - Piedicolle railway line and the Gorizia - Trieste and Gorizia - Udine lines, after the Armistice. The dark monochromatic color, perhaps gray-green, is curious

▼ Model 42 armored railway truck, used by the Germans after the Armistice, while carrying out the reversal maneuver, performed by hand by the crew (Paul Malmassari via Daniele Guglielmi)

AFTER THE ARMISTICE

Even in the Balkans, the day on which the Armistice signature was made public marked the beginning of a confusing transitional phase for all the Italian soldiers, perhaps even more confused than in other parts, because of the particular situation in which the armed forces were, scattered in a region where there were strong tensions with the many actors with which the Italians had to compete: the cumbersome German ally, the Croatian regular armed forces, the Slavic ethnic paramilitary movements, the well-organized Yugoslav partisan movement. Even in the Yugoslav territories the Italian armed forces reacted in different ways to the news of the Armistice: many units disbanded and their soldiers tried by all means to reach Italy, hoping for an end of the conflict, other units of the Royal Army instead did not give up their arms, but they continued to fight alongside their German ally or to join the Yugoslav liberation movement. In effect, the Armistice changed the military balance in the Balkan region, effectively leaving the territory out of control and offering a greater possibility of action to the partisans, who managed to reinforce their equipment with the equipment abandoned by the Italians.

At the time of the capitulation, the 2nd Army controlled the units of the Royal Army located in Slovenia and Croatia, up to the Neretva river in Herzegovina. The southernmost area, which included the Dubrovnik area, eastern Herzegovina, Montenegro, Kosovo, Western Macedonia and Albania, was the responsibility of the East Armada Group and the 3rd Army, while Istria and the Slovenian coast of the 8th Army. The situation of the armored units was as follows:

• Depending on the XI Army Corps, with headquarters in Ljubljana:

o   Autonomous Tank Company in Zara

o   Armored Car Company in Ljubljana

o   1st Battalion of the 31st Tanker Infantry Regiment (dependent on the "Lombardy" Division) with the 2nd Company in Jastrebarsko, the 3rd Company in Cronomelj and attached the 2nd Lanciafiamme Company

• From V Army Corps, with headquarters in Crikvenica, depended:

o   1st L Tanks Group "San Giusto", with its Squadrons distributed as we have seen in the previous chapters

• From the XIII Army Corps, divided between Split and Zadar, depended:

Tank Battalion of the 1st Division "Celere" in Split (the Division had moved to Sussak, but its units were still between Split and Knin)

• From the 6th Army Corps, with headquarters in Dubrovnik, depended:

o   2nd Tank Group

• From the XIV Army Corps in Montenegro depended:

o   3rd Battalion of the 31st Tanker Infantry Regiment.

The Armistice seized the Royal Army unprepared, although some units located in Dalmatia had begun to move towards national borders already during the summer and, even on 6th September, the "Isonzo" and "Lombardia" Divisions were reached by the order of fall back to Italy. Most of the Italian military was taken by a sense of dismay at the announcement of Badoglio and the most widespread desire among the soldiers was to reach the motherland in any way. As we have mentioned, in the days following the Armistice there were different reactions of the single Italian departments and some armored units disbanded, abandoning the materials and the means. Other units made the choice to oppose the German armed forces: in Dubrovnik the Italian units, including the 2nd Tank Group "San Marco", quickly organized a resistance against the SS Division "Prinz Eugen", which entered the city on September 13th. The German Division had moved from Herzegovina on 9th September and, having reached the Dalmatian city on the 13th, engaged in a furious battle on the city streets against the Italian garrison, which lasted over two hours. Despite the fierce defense, Italian troops had to capitulate and numerous L3 tanks and some old Lancia 1ZM armored cars were confiscated by the German military. The same situation was repeated a little everywhere in the Balkan peninsula: most of the abandoned armored vehicles were easy taken both to the People's Liberation Army of Yugoslavia, and to the German armed forces, and to the armored units of the Croatian Army. On the Adriatic coast at Crickvenica, for example, the Tito's partisans took over 1 M13/40 tank (with radiator problems, which were promptly solved), 3 AB41 armored cars and an AS37 protected truck, while in Knin the Germans requisitioned all armored cars abandoned by the Italians, especially light tanks and AS37 protected vehicles. The Germans, on the other hand, were already ready for a possible Italian defection from the month of August, fearing above all a collapse of Northern Italy and Italian Slovenia, easy nodes of access to the Reich from the south. On September 9th, the 19th SS Polizei Regiment disarmed the XI Army Corps in Ljubljana and the "Cacciatori delle Alpi" Division. Numerous AB41 armored cars and AS37 protected trucks were taken, which supplemented the armored vehicles of the Aufkl.Abt.17. A Battalion of the 1st SS Polizei Regiment of the a. SS Panzer Division LSSAH reached Trieste on 9th September and from there quickly proceeded to the occupation of Postumia, Pula, finally settling in the east on the old Italian-Yugoslav border. Emblematic of the general state of confusion that reigned among the Italian armed forces is represented by the case of Split, where the "Bergamo" Division was present, commanded by General Becuzzi, who also performed the functions of maximum civil authority. On September 10th, groups of Slavic partisans entered a city now in disarray, as Becuzzi was receiving contradictory orders from the High Command. At this juncture the General held an ambivalent attitude: on the one hand he tried to come to terms with the partisans, on the other he tried to make contact and deal with the German armed forces (which, moreover, had already subjected the city to bombing). The Slavic partisans soon discovered this double game and seized with the strength of Italian weapons and equipment, fearing that the latter would not oppose any attacks by the Germans. Thus, ended in the hands of the Slavs 16 tanks between L3 and L6 and at least 2 armored cars AB41. Split finally fell into chaos, even Croatian civilians took up arms from the soldiers of the Royal Army, arriving in some cases to humiliate them, stripping them of uniforms, while the Italian authorities quickly abandoned the city. After fierce fighting on September 25th, Split was occupied by the Germans, who shot 46 Italian officers, guilty of supporting the Slavic partisans.

In this confused state, only a part of the "San Giusto" Group and the 31st Carristi Regiment opted for the continuation of the war alongside the Germans and, as a result of the looting of the dispersed materials carried out by the other military forces present in the region, the units of the a newly formed Italian Social Republic was able to dispose of a small number of armored vehicles.

31st Tank Regiment

Some groups of Carri Veloci immediately supported the Germans in an open way and on the tanks they were painted white rectangles, with the long side vertically, as marks of recognition on the sides of the casemates and on the front of the vehicles. These were L3 tanks belonging to the 2nd Battalion of the 31st Tank Regiment. This Regiment, which had been transferred to Montenegro in July 1941, had 40 L3s tanks in charge at the time of the Armistice, some of which were flamethrowers, 8 old FIAT 3000 tanks, an unspecified number of L6/40s light tanks and some AB41 armored cars . Also the L6/40s of the unitt received the white rectangles, with the long side vertically, on the bow and on the back of the hull and on the sides of the blockhouse. On the front of the hull, next to the pilot's viewer, and on the rear hatch of the tower was a small lion's head, presumably painted after the tanks had been transferred to the Balkans.

In Podgorica the III Battalion was reached by the news of the Armistice, signed on September 8 in Cassibile. On September 10th Captain Ripandelli, commander of the 6th Company, with subordinate officers, gathered the ward and, accompanied by officers of the 5th Company and of the Command Company, gave a speech in which he declared that for the good of the Fatherland it was necessary to remain by his side of the Germans and continue the war, therefore asking those who wanted to continue to fight to take a step forward. Almost all of the Company adhered to the proposal of Captain Ripandelli and many officers and tankmen of the other Companies of the Battalion also joined. In the evening the 6th Company, together with the tank crews of the other Companies that had decided to continue fighting, moved to the clearing where the Germans were set aside. The military and tanks were thus framed in the 118. Jager – Division, in Podgorica, followed by other elements of both the II and the III Battalion. On the following days, many Italian soldiers who had fallen from other units also presented themselves at the Company's camp, asking to be enrolled. The Germans immediately prepared bilingual badges dated 9 September 1943 and then began collaboration with the Germans. The L3 tanks of the 3rd Battalion had a particular distinctive sign, a Balkenkreuz with double white corners on the sides of the casemates, and on the rear corners were given progressive white Arabic numerals on a light-colored rectangle, in place of the distinctive number of the Regiment. These were the only signs that identified the collaboration between the former allies, given that the tankers maintained the gray-green uniform, the insignia and the individual and collective armament. In November some L tanks participated in counter-insurgency operations with German units and in December a platoon participated in a mopping up action, which ended with the loss of 2 tanks, with fallen and wounded. After this operation the L tanks, while remaining always ready and available for use, remained still and were no longer used. Between the end of January and the beginning of February 1944, the order came to leave Podgorica to reach the Müsingen camp in Germany, with the aim of establishing an Armored

Battalion for the 1st Assault Division, which was however not never constituted, and the tankers went to form the Logistic Battalion of the Alpine Division "Monterosa". Thus, the history of the 3rd L Battalion of the 31st Regiment ended.

Armored Group "San Giusto"

The "San Giusto" Group was active in Venezia Giulia and in Istria, which originated from the 2nd "San Giusto" Light Tank Squadron of the 1st "Celere" Division. In the days immediately following the Armistice, under the command of Captain Agostino Tonegutti, a handful of men from Croatia reached Fiume with about fifteen L3 tanks, 4 of which were recovered during the march towards the redeemed city. After contributing to the defense of the city, on the German order, the "San Giusto" moved first to Gorizia (February 1944), where its staff were reinforced and received armored vehicles from the German Armed Forces, and finally to Mariano del Friuli (GO), in April of the same year. The unit, of the consistency of a Company, was definitively structured on Command, Squadron Command, M Tanks Squadron and L Tanks Squadron, with a maximum endowment of 35 armored vehicles of various types, all of Italian production, and a staff that reached 130 unit. The tasks entrusted to the unit were the escort to the logistic and military convoys in general, support to anti-partisan actions above all in support of German units, patrol of the communication routes and, occasionally, of the inhabited centers in the Gorizia, of the eastern Friuli and in the western Karst. In April 1945, due to the increasing pressure of the Yugoslav partisans towards Fiume, the Germans began to backtrack the front line and a substantial core of the "San Giusto" was consequently sent to the area of Rupa (now in Croatia), where, according to Germanic intentions, a position of resistance was being established. This operational unit of the Group, subjected to frequent attacks from the air, by Allied air formations, and from the ground, by the Tito's partisans, after having lost both men and tanks, retreated towards Trieste on the 27th, heading, the next day, to the Mariano del Friuli headquarters. Having arrived there, the Group had to acknowledge the fact that the "San Giusto" Depot, given the evolution of events, had already surrendered. The operative department therefore abandoned the armored vehicles (some of which were later used by the partisans against the German garrison of Cividale) and dissolved in the evening.

The symbol of the department was an italian tricolor flag, already applied in the first few months of the department's life; after the transfer to Mariano del Friuli in the center of the tricolor the outline of a black tank was painted, in its final version the tricolor was waving and it had in the center the black outline of a self-propelled on hull M.

The maximum equipment of the unit was made up of:

- 16 L3 light tanks

- 5 M tanks of variuous series

- 2 self propelled guns 47/32 L40

- 1 self propelled gun 75/18 M41

- 2 self propelled guns 75/18 M42

- 1 self propelled guns 75/34 M42

- 4 armored cars AB41

- 2 AS37 Protetto

- 2 FIAT 665NM Scudato

- 1 light truuck with artisanal protection.

The San Giusto Squadron Armored Group reached its definitive organization in the spring of 1944, structuring itself in this way:

- Command

- Command Squadron:

o Armored Cars Platoon

o Motorcycles Section

o Workshop Section

o Food and fuel Supply Section

o Vehicles

- M Tanks Squadron:

o Tanks Section

o Self-propelled Guns Section

o Motorcycles Section

- L Tanks Squadron:

o 1st Section

o 2 st Section

o 3 st Section

o Motorcycles Section

2nd Territorial Defense Militia Regiment "Istria"

The 2nd "Istria" Territorial Defense Militia Regiment was formed in Pola immediately after the Armistice, on three Companies and a Regimental Command Company "Mazza di Ferro", equipped with numerous vehicles, protected trucks and two L3 tanks. The Company "Mazza di Ferro" was based in Pula and it was initially commanded by Captain Bruno Artusi, former Lieutenant of the Bersaglieri; it was considered the Regiment's mobile department, because of the large availability of transport vehicles and armored vehicles. Captain Artusi was later replaced by Lieutenant Fausto Vardabasso, who, in turn, passed the command of the Company to Lieutenant Egidio Klausberg. The tasks of the "Mazza di Ferro" ("Iron Mace") were the escort to the vehicles columns, the prompt intervention and the connection between the republican garrisons of Istria. The light tanks of the department were two vehicles abandoned by the Royal Army at the time of the Armistice. One of the two was bought by an Istrian farmer, who had gathered a certain number of abandoned military vehicles in a kind of warehouse, paying 35,000 liras of the time, while the second tank was traded for... a truck loaded with shoes and clothing! One of the tanks, immobilized due to mechanical problems, was used as a buried fort at the entrance to the village of Buje and it was destroyed by the Legionaries of the unit on April 29th, 1945 with hand grenades, while the other was thrown at the end of the conflict in the port of Koper, fearing that it might fall into the hands of Tito's partisans. The Regiment established a widespread network of garrisons throughout Istria, which defended the civilian population from the infiltration of the Slavic partisans, who could only survive thanks to the auto-columns organized by the "Mazza di Ferro" Company. The Regiment, in fact, had an efficient garage that turned some trucks into protected vehicles, with metal plates, side shields fitted with slits and protective nets against hand-grenades, and armed them with coupled machine guns of 13.2 mm from the submarine, recovered at the great Arsenal of the Marina of Pola, or with machine guns from 20/65. These vehicles made it possible to carry out supplies of the garrisons scattered both along the coast and inland, escorting the columns that moved weekly to transport food. Some of these protected truckswere displaced, during the conflict, by the garrisons who were in the warmer areas. The armored vehicles of the "Mazza di Ferro" thus allowed to supply the scattered garrisons both along the coast and in the interior of Istria, escorting the columns that carried out this vital task weekly. The column was generally composed of one or two self-protected vehicles, trucks and a couple of motorcyclists, who preceded the vehicles to identify mines and explosive devices, which could have been placed on the roads by the partisans. It is difficult to establish precisely how many protected trucks were carried out for the "Iron Mace", even though some sources set the number of vehicles used by the Company at 6, including at least one FIAT 626 with the rears fitted for a FIAT 665 NM, a Lancia 3 armored RO and at least two FIAT 665 NM Scudato.

Others R.S.I.'s units
Another FIAT 665 NM Scudato, which was able to reconstruct the employment find trace, operated with the Friulian Volunteer Regiment "Tagliamento", received by the Command Company of the Regiment at the beginning of 1944, probably requisite at the Autocentro of Udine where it was in storage. The large truck, armed with an 8 mm machine gun, was frequently used to carry out daytime bets and patrols and it was made several times a sign of partisan attacks. During one of these ambushes, on 26th August 1944, it was hit by bullets of anti-tank rifle, immobilized and set on fire by the Slavic partisans. Also the XIV Army Coastal Defense Battalion, located in the Gorizia area, received a FIAT 665 NM armored truck, probably at the beginning of 1945, and was used until the end of the conflict for escorting convoys and was armed with a machine gun from 8 mm. The Bersaglieri Volunteer Battalion "Benito Mussolini", established in Verona and located in numerous fixed garrisons along the

Gorizia - Piedicolle railway, recovered a L40 self-propelled tank in early 1944. The vehicle was rarely used in support of the anti-partisan actions carried out by the department and after some months it was probably abandoned or given to another department, because it was not suitable for the type of war conducted by the department. Initially painted in yellow sand, the self-propelled was then camouflaged with large patches of dark green color.

Partisan's units with italian armored vehicles

As we have seen, in the days that followed the Armistice, the Yugoslav partisans recovered numerous armored vehicles of the Italian Royal Army, which had been abandoned by the Italian units disbanded or captured in combat. These armored vehicles went on to form real articulated armored units, a situation that it had no equal within the resistance movement in Italy. In Dalmatia, immediately after 8th September, some Italian soldiers switched to the Yugoslav resistance, bringing with them two L6/40 tanks, which were used in combat in the following months, losing the first during a battle and the second during an attack plane. The Slovenian Supreme Command instead managed to organize a Battalion on three Companies equipped with armored vehicles taken from the Italians in September 1943 in the border region; it consisted of 30 L3 and L6 tanks, 15 armored cars and 12 different armored vehicles (probably trucks with armor plating). After a few months of this huge booty only 10 tanks survived, especially L6, 6 armored cars and 4 armored vehicles, which were soon lost during clashes with the German Armed Forces. The Battalion was reconstituted in June 1944, thanks to other armored vehicles of Italian production captured in the area and in December it could have 6 L6/40, 3 L3 and 3 armored cars. After losing all the armored vehicles, the Battalion was once again constituted for the umpteenth time in March 1945, again with tanks of Italian production, and participated in the clashes of the last days of the war, entering Ljubljana on 9th May. A Battalion composed of two Armored Companies and a Command and Service was set up with 16 tanks between L3 and L6 and 2 AB41 captured in Split. The Companies were employed in Dalmatia and Croatia, but most of the vehicles were lost, destroyed or captured by the Germans, during the reconquest of Split. With the three surviving tanks an armored section was formed within the 1st Yugoslav Proletarian Division, a section that operated in various areas of the country. In the autumn of 1944, the L3 and L6 survivors were confiscated by the V Yugoslav Corpus, which included them in an Armored Company, along with other Italian and French vehicles captured. The "Lazo Marin" Company, named after its first commander, entered Zagreb on May 9th, 1945. Even groups of Italian tankers after 8th September 1943 agreed with the local resistance movements, opposing the Germans, as happened both in Albania and Yugoslavia, where about 40,000 Italians took part in the war for the liberation of Yugoslavia. Let us remember, by way of example, that already on 7th September 1943, two L6/40s went to the 13th Proletarian Brigade "Rade Koncar". The two light tanks, which probably belonged to the 2nd Company of the 1st Battalion of the 31st Infantry Infantry Regiment deployed in the Croatian town of Jastrebarsko, were placed in an armored unit dependent on the I Korpus of the People's Liberation Army of Yugoslavia and subsequently employed in combat by the Italian crews.

Croatian and Slovenian units equipped with Italian tanks

On 10th April 1941, four days after the German invasion of Yugoslavia, Croatia declared itself an independent state, governed by a government led by Ante Pavelic, head of the pro-fascist political-military organization of the Ustaša. Croatia, obviously an ally of Germany and Italy, quickly organized Armed Forces: the day after the independence declaration, the Croatian National Guard (Hrvastko Domobranstvo) was created, dependent on the Ministry of Defense. On 16th April, the actual Armed Forces were organized, consisting of the Army (Kopnena Vojska), the Air Force (Zrakoplovstvo Nezavisne Drzave Hrvatske) and the Gendarmerie (Hrvastko Oružništvo). However, the Ustašas found themselves in a prominent paramilitary training position, very similar, in Pavelic's intentions, to the Waffen SS. The vastness and nature of the predominantly mountainous Croatian territory, and the need to keep both Titian partisans and Mihailovic Cetnians at bay were the reasons that led the military authorities to organize armored infantry support units, asking Germany for armored vehicles and to Italy. In the spring of 1941, Germany supplied the Ustaša with a certain number of tanks of little war value (Polish tankets and old Renault FT17, war prey of the dissolved Yugoslav army) and only in December 4 Panzer I, while Italy supplied 15 L3 tanks. In the following years the offensive potential of the Ustaša was increased, aggregating an armored Company to each of the first 5 Ustaša Brigades, each equipped with 2/6 italian light tank. In the same period, 4 Mountain Brigades and 4 Jäger Brigades were also being organized and each of these should have had a Tank Platoon, consisting of 3 medium tanks and 2 light tanks.

With the capitulation of Italy following the Armistice, the Croats managed to grab 26 L6/40 light tanks and an unknown number of self-propelled 47/32 L40, lying in the Italian deposits of the Dalmatian coast; a dozen of L6/40 were captured by the Ustašas in the areas of Jastrebarsko and Karlovac; in December the Germans supplied other material, selling 13 L3 wagons, prey of the Armistice, to the IV Ustaša Brigade. Photographic evidence allows us to assert with certainty that the Pavelic militia also had at least one AB41 armored car and FIAT666 NM shielded trucks, although these vehicles do not appear in any official document. From the end of 1943, the Ustaša armored units were mainly used in three areas: in the south-west and north of Zagreb (Zagoje) and in the sector of Gospic.

At the beginning of 1944, the Mountain and Jäger Brigades were also equipped with Italian L3 tanks, and in the spring of the '44 the Germans ceded 4 Italian L40 self-propelled vehicles, which went to equip the Pavelic Guard Artillery Regiment. In November, Ante Pavelic decided the merger between the Army and the Ostaša Vojnica, which now held the record in terms of military potential, in a unitary armed force, the Hrvastke Oruzane Snege, while the Poglavnik Guard maintained its independence. The Mobile Army Regiment merged into the Armored Company of the Guard of the Poglavnik, which went more and more to assume the structure of a mechanized Division, becoming in January 1945 Poglavnikova Tjelesna Divjzia (P.T.D.).

The first months of 1945 saw an increase in the pressure intensity of the Tito's partisans and, consequently, the commitment of the Croatian armored units multiplied. By direct order of Pavelic, in the first days of May the bulk of the Croatian Armed Forces was concentrated in Zagreb; the order was to move to Austria, so as to escape the Tito's vise. In addition to ones of the P.T.D., other tanks were also restored during the repair phase, so as to ensure effective protection during the planned folding. Supporting heavy fighting, the Croats reached the Austrian border on May 14th, where the last fights were supported. The survivors were concentrated in the British prison camp of Grafenstein, near Klagenfurt, but many of them were later taken by Yugoslav partisans and many soldiers were handed over for weapons.

The Croatian armored units that received Italian tanks were:

• Tank Company of the 1st Brigata Ustaša

• Tank Company of the 3rd Ustaša Brigade

• Tank Company of the 4th Ustaša Brigade

• Tank company of the 5th Ustaša Brigade

• Tank Companies of P.T.B.

• Ustaša Obrana (Mobile Unit of Defense Ustaša)

• 1st Company Light Tanks of the 1st Mountain Division

• Tank Platoon of the 1st Mountain Brigade

• Tank Platoon of the 3rd Mountain Brigade

• Tank Platoon of the 4th Mountain Brigade

• Tank Platoon of the 3rd Jäger Brigade

• Tank Platoon of the 4th Jäger Brigade

• Armored Reserve Company (also referred to as Reserve Armored Command)

• Light Tank Platoon of the 1st Transport Battalion

In September 1943, following the Italian surrender, Slovenia was occupied by German troops, passing under the direct dependencies of the Gauleiter of Carinthia Rainer. In the same month of September, a collaborationist militia with a predominantly voluntary nature was created, the Slovenian Territorial Guard (Slovensko Domobranstvo), to support the German Armed Forces in contrast to the E.P.J., commanded by Leon Rupnik, former general of the Yugoslav army; it was equipped by the Germans with weapons seized from the Italians after the Armistice of 1943 and it was trained by the German SS. At the end of the summer of 1944 the Domobranci received from the Germans an unspecified number of self-propelled vehicles from L40 to 47/32, some of which were of late production, that is with the casemate modified and enlarged, and armed with a Breda 38 machine gun with shielding. The tanks were used by units located in the Lubliana area; according to a partisan document at the end of 1944 the Domobranci had 6 "tanks", probably all self-propelled L40 and employed by the Ordnungspolizei Pol. Pz. Kp. 14. The Domobranci also used trucks with Italian armored armor plating and they supplied crews for some armored trains operating in Slovenia.

▲ In the Balkans, on the same day the Armistice signing was made, some armored units of the Royal Army continued to fight alongside the German departments; in the photo, a self-propelled 75/18 with Italian crew during an action with German soldiers in the Balkans (B.A.)

▼ A L3 tank flamethrower abandoned in the park of Split after the battles in the days following the Armistice (Crippa)

▲ Italian tanks in support of German units in the days following the Armistice

▲ The light tanks of the II Battalion of the 31st Tanks Regiment received white rectangles, with the long side vertically, as an identifying symbol for the vehicles that operated in collaboration with the German military after the Armistice in the Balkans (B.A.)

▼ Some L3 tanks of the II Battalion of the 31st Tanks Regiment support German soldiers after the Armistice during an anti-partisan operation (B.A.)

▲ Tank officers of the II Battalion of the 31st Tank Regiment in conversation with a German officer. Behind them an L6/40 tank of the unit (B.A.)

▼ L6/40 tank of the II Battalion of the 31st Tanks Regiment engaged in the recovery of a German truck. Note the lion's head painted on the front of the blockhouse and the white rectangles, with a long vertical side, typical of the tanks of this unit that supported the German armed forces after the Armistice (B.A.)

▲ Armored car AB41 of the III Battalion of the 31st Tanks Regiment patrolling the hills of Montenegro, in support of a group of German soldiers, in the days following the Armistice (B.A.)

▼ A L3 of the 6th Company of the III Tanks Battalion supports the advance of a Germanic Jager unit in Montenegro in late September 1943 (B.A.)

▲ Beautiful snapshot of a tank man of the III Battalion of the 31st Regiment, who continued to fight alongside the Germans in Montenegro after the Armistice; note the stars on the collar (B.A.)

▲ Another chariot of the same Battalion in support of a unit of German Alpine troops (B.A.)

▼ L3/33 tanks of the III Battalion of the 31st Tanks Regiment in Montenegro after the Armistice. The mimetic coloring with green spots on a brown background and the Arabic number in white are clearly visible, on a lighter background than the rest of the wagon, probably yellow, at the corners of the casamate (Crippa)

▲ German soldiers observe the effects of artillery fire on enemy positions, protected by two L3 tanks and an AB41 armored car from the III Battalion of the 31st Tanks Regiment (B.A.)

▼ One of the L3/35 light floats of the III Battalion of the 31st Tanks Regiment in Niksic after 8th September (Ratti)

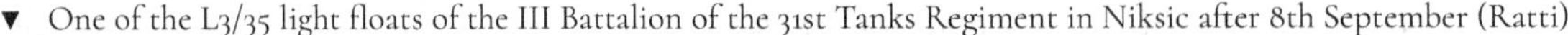

▲ Self-propelled 75/34 of the Armored Group "San Giusto" in the original sand-colored livery, detail that makes the photo date to the second half of 1944, when it was delivered to the unit (Arena)

▲ L3 of the Squadroni Corazzati "San Giusto" filmed in the courtyard of the Industrial School of Mariano del Friuli (GO), site of the unit, in the autumn of 1944. On the machine-gun shielding is depicted the coat of arms while on the sides of the casemate are still present the tactical symbols of the Royal Army (Benvenuti - Colonna)

▼ In the autumn of 1944, many vehicles of the "San Giusto" received a very complex camouflage, made with a dense network of brown and green spots on the sand-yellow background, like this M13/40 tank, which bears, next to the pilot's viewer, the tricolor waving with the black wagon, the latest version of the emblem. Finally, the presence of the two spare guide rollers on the front bumpers is curious

▲ Close-up photograph of the same tank of the previous photograph, which allows us to appreciate the complex mimetic scheme and the crest of the "San Giusto" Group in its final configuration (Viziano)

▼ M13/40 and self-propelled 75/34 of the "San Giusto" at the end of 1944, both with the new camouflage coloring; the self-propelled does not have the Group symbol, as instead the tank has, next to the position of the machine guns (Arena)

▲ One of the two self-propelled 47/32 of the "San Giusto" Group in the countryside of Mariano del Friuli (GO) in February 1945. The vehicle appears heavily camouflaged (Pisanò)

▼ Trucks R.S.I. in the square of Koper in November 1943 during a demonstration in favor of the newly reconstituted Army. In the foreground, a FIAT 626 from the "Mazza di Ferro" Company, which was fitted with armor plating of the larger FIAT 665 NM Scudato, camouflaged in the classic three colors yellow sand, brown and green (M.N.Z.)

▲   Two FIAT 665NM armored trucks probably of the "Mazza di Ferro" Company of the 2nd M.D.T. Regiment in Istria. The camouflage at the edges of the first half is interesting, as is the presence of a hand-made turret on both trucks (Crippa)

▼ Yugoslav partisans celebrating around a L3 just captured near the walls of Spalato (Crippa)

▲ One L6/40 of the 3rd Battalion of the 31st Tank Regiment, of which the symbol on the casemate is recognized, just captured by the titans immediately after the Armistice (Crippa)

▼ The first of these two L6/40, finished in the hands of the Croatian partisans, still bears the head of Mickey Mouse, symbol of the Battalion of the Royal Army, and the plaque "RE 5219" (Crippa)

▲ Armored car AB41 of the Armored Battalion of the Split's partisans; the machine has the typical Italian three-color camouflage (brown and green spots on a sandy yellow background) and curiously bears spare wheels with "Libya" tires, although "Artiglio" tires are mounted on the vehicle (Crippa)

▼ Section of tankkettes L3 of N.O.V.H. Tenkbatalion, a Tank Battalion constituted by the E.P.J.L. in Croatia (Crippa)

▲ AS37 armored truck taken by Slavic partisans, to whom additional superior protection was applied (Crippa)

▼ A group of Yugoslav partisans laying on a light tank L3 caught at Italian units after the Armistice (Crippa)

▲ The same tank of the previous photo in gear: note the lack of machine guns (Crippa)

▲ A tank L6/40 used by the Tito's partisans (Crippa)

▲ An armored section of the Yugoslav People's Liberation Army consisting of an L3 and an L6 tank. (Crippa)

▼ Soldiers of the Yugoslav People's Liberation Army photographed in Trieste at the end of the conflict. There is also an Italian CV33 tankette, apparently repainted in a light color, perhaps sand (Arena)

▲ After the Armistice in the Balkans the German armed forces seized numerous tanks abandoned by the Italian units and reused them in the struggle against the Slavic partisans, like this L6/40 (Benvenuti - Colonna)

▲ The photo probably depicts one of the Lancia armored cars captured by the Germans in Dubrovnik, at the end of the clashes that took place in the city against the L Tank Group "San Marco" on September 13th, 1943

▼ A tank of the 16.Polizei-Panzer Kompanie, formed in June 1944 in Croatia and equipped with 8 L3 tankettes and 2 self-propelled L40

▲ On the cover of this magazine dedicated to the Ustaša, one of the L6/40 light tanks captured by Pavelic's formation appears in the days immediately following the Armistice

▲ Although not mentioned in the documents, this photograph testifies to the use by units of the Ustaša of Italian armored cars AB41. The fact that the vehicle is not used by the units of 369. or 373. (Kroatische) Infanterie-Division, dependent by the German Armed Forces, who were in charge of this type of armored car, is testified by the presence, on the rear of the blockhouse, of the typical symbol of Pavelic's formation. This armored vehicle, taken up in Varazdin in 1944, would in fact belong to the 3rd Armored Company of P.T.B.

▲ L3 tank's column of a Ustaša Brigade in winter 1943; we appreciate the entirely green coloring of the carts and the emblem of Pavelic's formation on the front lining of the L3s

▼ Column of tanks L6/40 and of Italian trucks, used by the Ustashas, in the main street of a Croatian village

▲ Self-propelled by Domobranci during the swearing-in ceremony in the Ljubljana stadium. The tank in the background seems to have the casemate of the first type, not enlarged and it is evident that the patches of the camouflage are of two colors, probably brown and green

BIBLIOGRAPHY

- Barlozzetti Ugo, Pirella Alberto, *"Mezzi dell'Esercito italiano 1935 – 1945"*, Editoriale Olimpia, Firenze, 1986.
- Benvenuti Bruno, Colonna Ugo, *"Fronte Terra"* volumi 1, 2/I, 2/II e 2/III, Edizioni Bizzarri, Roma 1974.
- Campini Dino, *"Nei giardini del Diavolo"*, Longanesi, Milano, 1969.
- Cappellano Filippo, Pignato Nicola, *"Gli autoveicoli da combattimento dell'Esercito Italiano"*, volumi I e II, S.M.E. – Ufficio Storico, Roma, 2002.
- Ceva Lucio, Curami Andrea, *"La meccanizzazione dell'Esercito fino al 1943"*, S.M.E – Ufficio Storico, Roma, 1989.
- Corbatti Sergio, Nava Marco, *"Come il diamante"*, Laran Editions, Bruxelles, 2008.
- Crippa Paolo, *"I mezzi corazzati italiani della guerra civile 1943-1945"*, Mattioli 1885, Fidenza (PR), 2015.
- Crippa Paolo, *"I Reparti Corazzati della Repubblica Sociale Italiana 1943 -1945"*, Marvia Edizioni, Voghera (PV), 2006.
- Crippa Paolo, *"Italia 43-45 - I blindati di circostanza della guerra civile"*, Mattioli 1885, Fidenza (PR), 2014.
- Cucut Carlo, *"Le Forze Armate della R.S.I. 1943 – 1945 – Forze di terra"*, G.M.T., Trento, 2005.
- De Lorenzis Ugo, *"Dal primo all'ultimo giorno. Ricordi di guerra 1939 - 1945"*, Longanesi, Milano, 1971.
- Di Colloredo Mels Pierluigi Romeo, *"Controguerriglia – La 2° Armata italiana e l'occupazione dei Balcani 1941 – 1943"*, Luca Cristini Editore, 2019, Bergamo.
- Giusti Maria Teresa, Rossi Aga, *"Una guerra a parte. I militari italiani nei Balcani, 1940-1945"*, Il Mulino, Bologna, 2017.
- Panetta Rinaldo, *"Il ponte di Klisura. I carristi italiani in Albania 1940 – 1941"*, Mursia, Milano, 1975.
- Pignato Nicola, *"Motori!!! Le truppe corazzate italiane 1919 – 1994"*, GMT, Trento, 1995.
- Pignato Nicola, *"Un secolo di autoblinde in Italia"*, Mattioli 1885, Parma, 2008.
- Pisanò Giorgio, *"Gli ultimi in grigioverde"*, Edizioni F.P.E., Milano, 1967.
- Predoević Dinko, Dimitrijević Bojan, *"Oklopne postrojbe Sila Osovine na jugoistoku Europe u Drugome svjetskom ratu"*, Despot Infinitus d.o.o., Zagabria (Croazia), 2015.

TITOLI PUBBLICATI - ALREADY PUBLISHING

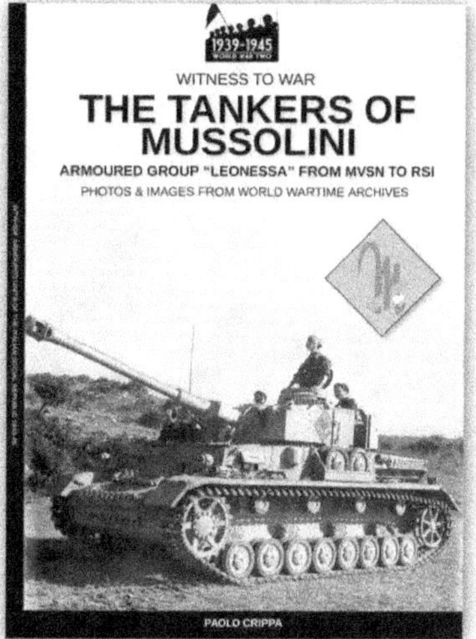

SOLDIERSHOP
PUBLISHING
BOOKS TO COLLECT